PUFFIN BOOKS

UK | USA | Canada | Ireland | Australia
India | New Zealand | South Africa

Puffin Books is part of the Penguin Random House group of companies
whose addresses can be found at global.penguinrandomhouse.com.

www.penguin.co.uk
www.puffin.co.uk
www.ladybird.co.uk

Penguin
Random House
UK

First published in Australia by Penguin Random House Australia Pty Ltd 2019
Published in Great Britain by Puffin Books 2021

001

Printed and bound in Great Britain by Clays Ltd, Elcograf S.p.A

The authorized representative in the EEA is Penguin Random House Ireland,
Morrison Chambers, 32 Nassau Street, Dublin D02 YH68

A CIP catalogue record for this book is available from the British Library

ISBN: 978–0–241–43493–2

All correspondence to:
Puffin Books
Penguin Random House Children's
One Embassy Gardens,
8 Viaduct Gardens
London SW11 7BW

MIX
Paper from
responsible sources
FSC
www.fsc.org   FSC® C018179

Penguin Random House is committed to a
sustainable future for our business, our readers
and our planet. This book is made from Forest
Stewardship Council® certified paper.

GAVIN AUNG THAN

SUPER
SIDE
KICKS

Trial of Heroes

PREVIOUSLY ...

Four superhero sidekicks were sick of being bullied by their selfish grown-up partners, so they decided to form their own team. They are the

SUPER SIDEKICKS!

JUNIOR JUSTICE (JJ to his friends)

Born leader. Expert martial artist. Brilliant detective. Assisted by Ada, the world's most advanced belt buckle.

FLYGIRL

Acrobatic flyer. Bug whisperer. Cricket lover (the sport and the insect). Uses dangerous bug balls to subdue enemies.

DINOMITE

Dinosaur shapeshifter. Physics professor. Poetry connoisseur. Would rather be reading a book.

GOO

Limitless stretch factor. Untapped power potential. Still has nightmares about his past as a bad guy.

THE GROWN-UPS

Captain Perfect, the world's most beloved (and obnoxious) superhero; **Rampagin' Rita**, simple yet scary strong; and **Blast Radius**, who hasn't met a problem he couldn't solve by blowing it up.

Chapter

3

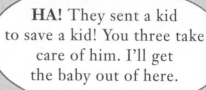

11

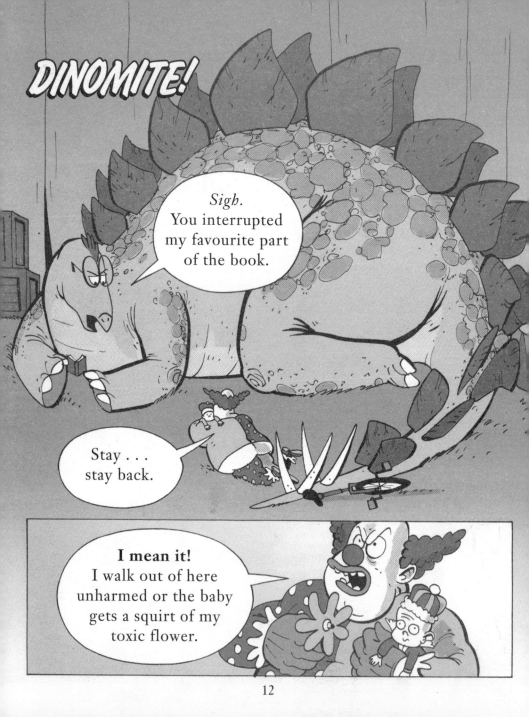

Sir Laughs-a-lot. **Real name:** Frederick Golinski.

Height: 182 centimetres. **Weight:** 123 kilograms. Suffers from onset of pre-diabetes and heart disease.

Tsk tsk, too many of those carnival snacks, Frederick? Also allergic to **eggs**, **aspirin** and **bee stings**.

. . . anything?

THOK THOK THOK

Yeah, so? What does that have to do with . . .

* As seen in SUPER SIDEKICKS book 2! – Gav

18

Chapter

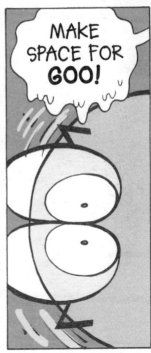

Aren't you coming in, JJ? You deserve a break.

Some of us have work to do, Flygirl. There's so much admin stuff to catch up on.

We've been invited to **open a shopping mall** in Shanghai, Tiamata* wants a report on the amount of **ocean plastic that's been cleaned** and now the Queen wants us to **guard the royal baby** during their visit here!

* We met Tiamata, Mother of the Seas, in SUPER SIDEKICKS book 2. – Gav

Plus, I'm still waiting to hear from H.E.R.O.* about why our membership wasn't approved.

Relax, mate, that stuff isn't important.

* Heroic Earth Righteousness Organization

23

The **Heroic Earth Righteousness Organization** just happens to be the most prestigious superhero club on the planet.

All the greatest superheroes were members: The Caped Invader. Amy Amazon. Green Nightlight. **Even Johnny Jingo!**

Sounds like a cult if you ask me.

Being inducted is the highest honour a superhero can receive and will give us **instant credibility!** Dinomite, refuel the jet . . .

. . . the Super Sidekicks **are going to New York!**

Sigh. I knew I'd have to get out of the pool.

New York City, USA.

Flying in their new **Technodactyl**, a supersonic plastic-fueled jet capable of speeds of mach 9*, the Super Sidekicks reach their destination in only a few hours.

* Nine times the speed of sound.

How's she handling, Ada? I adjusted the horizontal stabiliser before we left.

Pitch and roll are stable, Dinomite. She flies like a dream.

Look, there it is . . .

29

Facial scans accepted. Good afternoon, Super Sidekicks. Welcome to the Heroic Earth Righteousness Organization. Please proceed to level eighty-three.

Impressive.

You don't understand, team. I've wanted to be a H.E.R.O. member ever since I first wore my underpants on the outside. **This is a dream come true for me.**

And the stories about the Director are **legendary.** He founded this place in 1952 after defeating the giant Cyclord and saving New York. That made him the most admired hero in the world.

I can't believe we're going to meet him in person.

Look, it's Flash Jordan's battle blaster!

He used that to fight off the Martian invasion of 1938. I bet those Martians never stood a chance.

And this is Wonder Lady's **laxative lasso!**

She would tie criminals up and her magical lasso would force them to poop their pants.

Ew! I hope they washed that thing.

Highly unsanitary.

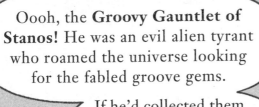

Oooh, the **Groovy Gauntlet of Stanos!** He was an evil alien tyrant who roamed the universe looking for the fabled groove gems.

If he'd collected them all he would have become the **funkiest villain** in the galaxy.

Thankfully the **Disco Squad** stopped him in 1979.

Well, well, well. Look who made it.

Hey, Captain, why didn't you ever nominate me to be a H.E.R.O. member when I was your sidekick?

Oh, it's no myth, my young friends!

Sir.

I was awarded that in 1948, and it gave me my ability to **harness electricity.** That's how I defeated the mighty Cyclord and saved New York City.

It's you . . . I can't believe it's really you.

You're too kind, my boy! Now allow me to introduce myself. I am the Director of this fine organization, but most know me by my hero name . . .

It's such an honour to –

HA HA HA! Super Supreme! That's your name, for real?

Hello, Pizza House? Can I order a large Super Supreme? Hold the pineapple.

Quiet! You dare insult the Director?!

Forgive my teammates, sir. They don't realize the importance of the occasion.

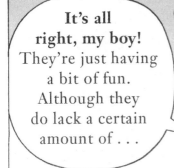

It's all right, my boy! They're just having a bit of fun. Although they do lack a certain amount of . . .

. . . respect.

Captain Perfect mentioned you've reviewed our membership application.

Yes, I've been watching you from afar.

Some splendid superhero work your team has been doing.

That's why it pains me so much to say that while I'm flattered by your interest in joining H.E.R.O. . . .

. . . I'm afraid membership is **not open to children.**

But . . . but . . . surely we've proven ourselves worthy.

Policy is policy, I'm afraid.

The Trial of Heroes.

An ancient test of **one's true heroism.** A series of challenges so dangerous, no one besides myself has completed it in more than a century.

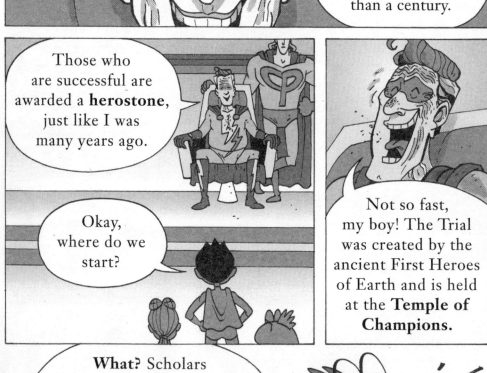

Those who are successful are awarded a **herostone**, just like I was many years ago.

Okay, where do we start?

Not so fast, my boy! The Trial was created by the ancient First Heroes of Earth and is held at the **Temple of Champions.**

What? Scholars have been trying to find the Temple of Champions for hundreds of years. It's thought to be a legend, like El Dorado or the lost city of Atlantis.

You are a clever one, aren't you? I found the Temple as a young man, and I can assure you it is **very real** and even more breathtaking than the legends describe.

If the four of you pass the Trial of Heroes, then I will fully admit that your age is irrelevant and you deserve to be members of H.E.R.O.

In fact, if you return with the herostone I will grant all of you **lifetime platinum status.**

Wow, platinum!

But, sir, I've been a member for years and I'm still only bronze status!

Perhaps your status would improve if you attempted the Trial **yourself**, Captain.

Uh-uh, that temple gives me the creeps!

We can do it, sir. I'm sure of it.

Splendid. **That's the spirit!**

Excuse me, Super Pepperoni, do you mind if we have a word with JJ?

This really means that much to you? Risking our lives to get into some club?

It's for *us*! Membership will mean we get fully accepted as legit superheroes. No more getting teased because we're young. No more getting laughed at by the media.

Dinomite, what do you reckon?

If the Director is telling the truth, then bringing back evidence of the Temple of Champions would be a **major archaeological discovery.**

After **everything** Junior Justice do for Goo, Goo follow Junior Justice **anywhere!**

Thanks, buddy.

Fine, fine. It looks like I'm outnumbered, and as I've said before: **we stick together, always.**

It'll be worth it, Flygirl, I promise.

* A region stretching from modern-day Egypt to Iran. – Gav

Chapter

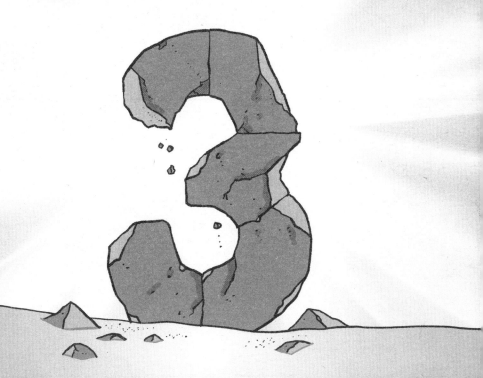

The First Heroes of Earth. An ancient society where every citizen had superpowers. They built a thriving civilization devoted to **equality and justice.**

So what happened?

CLICK

No one knows for sure. But some believe there were a few survivors, and that those descendants are the superheroes alive today.

55

And you . . . let me guess. You're the loveable goofball of the team?

I'll have you know I've been shortlisted for the Nobel Prize!

No, Goo loveable goofball!

My mistake. I wish I'd known you were coming. This place is an **absolute mess.** Here, let me clean up a bit.

Yes, guarding this temple is a thankless task, but someone's got to do it!

SWEEP SWEEP

SWEEP

Very well then. The Trial is made up of **three challenges.** Each tests one of the **Pillars of Heroism.** Complete the Trial and you shall be rewarded with a **herostone** – a sacred gift that will grant you **any superpower you wish.**

The three Pillars of Heroism . . . what are they?

You will find out soon enough. Or then again, **maybe you won't.**

Now go, Super Sidekicks. **The Trial of Heroes awaits!**

59

62

THUNK!

Ugh, hot. It's so hot.

My wings!!! Why don't I have my wings?!

Goo cannot move!

Ocean fire.

Huh? What did you –

65

You're right, you're right. I'm sorry. I got you all into this mess.

But the door we came in from is sealed. The only way out is across the pit.

Look, we knew this was going to be hard, but if we're going to get out of here alive, we're going to have to do it **together.**

I only agreed to come here because you're the **bravest heroes** I know and there's no one else I'd rather have by my side doing this Trial than **you three.**

Now, Super Sidekicks, **ARE YOU WITH ME?!**

Pretty good speech.

He has a gift.

All right, fine, we're with you. But what about Goo? He's useless like this.

Goo cannot move!

Mmm, he can't stretch himself, but maybe we can do it for him.

If we just pull out two of these like so.

How do we look?

Beautiful!

I don't believe this. I'm a dinosaur of science, not some **hopscotching kangaroo.**

Slow down, JJ. Don't get too cocky!

AH! I didn't realize how much I depend on my wings.

It's too far, Dinomite. Jump, and I'll catch you.

Egh!

I . . . can't. I depend on my shapeshifting power to solve any physical problem. **This is too much.**

69

GOTCHA!

AHHH!

SSsSSSsssSS

Forget about it, just get up here!

I owe you my life, Flygirl.

We'll treat your wound once we're safe, Dinomite. Just move carefully . . .

. . . I'm not sure how long these pillars are going to hold.

71

Dang it, Bakoo, you scared us!

Apologies, Super Sidekicks!

You wouldn't believe the number of heroes who have fallen to their fiery death here.

My wings are back!

Goo stretchy again.

Ada! I missed you.

Error alert! My activity log is missing the last sixteen minutes of time. Scanning for viruses.

It wasn't a virus, Ada. You vanished then reappeared out of thin air. What kind of **unknown science** is this?!

Not science. Magic. **Ancient magic.**

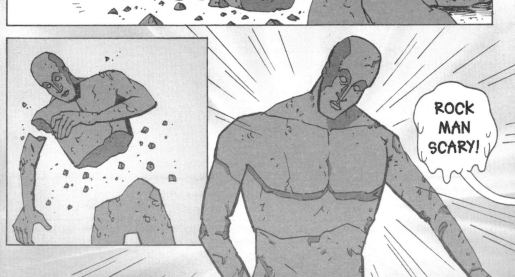

93

What's it doing?

You've gotta be kidding me!

Aw, poop!

Goo no like rock man!

SPLA-KOOSH!

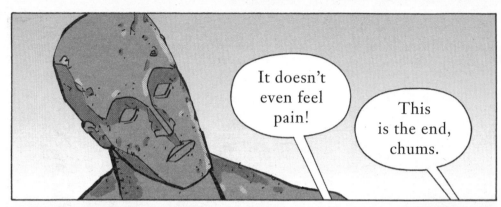

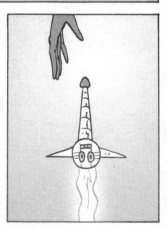

BRAVO!

Stop doing that, Bakoo!

It . . . it's finally dead?

Yes! The man of stone takes thirty-three kills to be defeated.

Many more powerful and experienced heroes than you have faced him. But they gave up too easily. They lacked one thing which you four have just demonstrated: **PERSISTENCE!**

That is the second **Pillar of Heroism.** The will to not give up against overwhelming odds. The tenacity to get back up again and again, no matter the challenge. **That is what a true hero does.**

Be prepared for anything.

Over there! The herostone symbol.

That's where the final challenge must be.

What's that smell?

Kind of like wet –

Eww! Goo, don't get your slime on me!

Not Goo slime...

No hurt friends!

CROR GRRA

Hurry, Super Sidekicks, run away!

Goo love puppy. Goo love –

CHOMP!

There's something nasty stuck in there. **We have to help him, JJ!**

What?! Look how vicious he is!

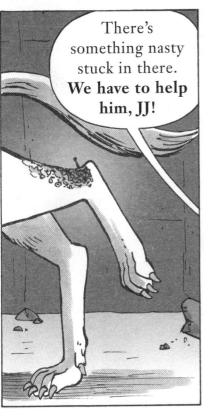

He needs help. The poor thing must be in agony.

We're meant to defeat him, not get eaten!

Flygirl is right. I won't stand for an animal being in pain.

You two apply first aid while I hold the canine down.

How are you going to do that?!

FHOOF!

I mean you no harm, chum, but I must subdue you.

COUGH!

Fun ride in puppy mouth!

THOOM THOOM THOOM

BOOM BOOM BOOM

KLAMP!

Goo, wrap the dog's back legs!

I can't thank you enough, Super Sidekicks. That silly sword has been stuck in Goliath's paw for more than **one hundred years!**

The poor boy was driven completely feral with pain, and every warrior who makes it this far always tries to **fight him.** They think this is a challenge of **muscle and brawn.**

No, this is a challenge of **compassion and empathy!** A true hero would have seen the pain he was in and helped. Just like **you** did.

For **kindness** in a hero is just as important as strength.

Chapter

Bakoo, is that you?

You're immortal?

Yes, this is my **true appearance.** I am the only remaining First Hero, left behind to guard and protect the Temple of Champions.

Not quite, but as long as the Temple is here then so shall I be, watching over it.

If you were here, why didn't you help Goliath yourself?

I'm forbidden to **interfere** with the challenges. He had to be helped by a Trial champion.

You don't know how long I've been waiting for champions like you to help my precious boy.

Besides, I'd prefer to know that my intellect is **earned** rather than given to me by some magic stone.

What about you, Goo?

Goo **happy** way Goo is!

You should be the one to use it, JJ. You don't have any superpowers.

Mmmm ...I don't know.

Let me think about it. I've always prided myself on being a superhero **without** superpowers. It kind of **defines who I am.**

I'm just glad we earned this thing **together.** I knew we could do it.

Use it wisely. That is the first herostone I've awarded in over a century.

You forgot **Super Supreme.** He completed the Trial in 1948, remember?

I'm afraid you are **mistaken.** I do not know who you're talking about.

What?! He's the Director of H.E.R.O. – the Heroic Earth Righteousness Organization! That's the whole reason we're here. Super Supreme promised us membership if we brought back a herostone, just like he did.

Interesting. 1948, you said? The Temple has a memory of everyone who has been here.

1948

But Super Supreme is a **living legend!** He founded H.E.R.O. for the good of the superhero community, as a tribute to all that they've done. If you're right, then it's all a lie. **A complete sham.**

I knew it was a cult!

Naughty old man.

I'm sorry, mate.

Never blindly follow those in power, Junior Justice. Make them **earn** your **respect** and **loyalty.**

Better you learn this lesson now, while you're still young.

It's been a **pleasure,** Super Sidekicks. I shall miss you.

Goo says bye bye!

Farewell, my young champions.

Thanks for everything, Bakoo. Maybe we can come back and visit. You must get lonely here.

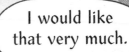

I would like that very much.

Here, you can have this. It's a **Playtendo** game console. It's loaded with heaps of games that will keep you busy for a while.

SWEET!

No way – they did it.

Um . . . uh . . . **WELCOME BACK,** young heroes!

I, uh . . . see that you successfully completed the Trial. **Very impressive.** I had no doubts! Now, if you just hand over the herostone, I will gladly give you all **lifetime platinum membership** here.

Captain Perfect, have you ever actually seen Super Supreme do anything **heroic** or use his powers?

Of course! There was that time he . . . um . . . you know, when he fought . . . uh . . .

He defeated Cyclord in 1951: **everyone knows that!**

Anyone can have a **painting commissioned and spread lies in the media.** I'll ask you again: have you ever seen Super Supreme use his powers?

I should not have to prove myself to children, but if you insist. **Is this satisfactory?**

I'm guessing you have some kind of **miniature tesla coil** built into your gloves. Nothing but a harmless light show.

You would normally be punished for such **disrespect.** But if you just hand over that herostone, **all will be forgiven,** children.

Don't you get it, Captain? Super Supreme has been **lying to us all along.** He's not a superhero – he never has been! H.E.R.O., all of this, **is a lie.**

He's just been trying to get his hands on a herostone for all these years so he could have a real superpower.

Have you lost your mind? **He passed the Trial!** He already has a herostone!

Why don't you tell him the truth, Super Supreme?

That you had a little **pee-pee accident** in the Courage Pit.

132

138

139

140

The herostone, JJ!
USE THE HEROSTONE!

What? I . . . I forgot all about it.

I don't even know where it is. It got knocked out of my hands.

Goo catch stone, keep it safe.

Yes!

Okay, um . . . let's see . . . I want the power to save Dinomite.

I do feel bad, chum. Using the herostone to save me means you will **never** be able to give yourself a superpower.

Don't be silly. I can't think of a better way to have used it.

After all, you **did** jump in front of that blaster shot for me.

All I know is my whole body is still sore from fighting the man of stone. Sheesh, that thing was scary.

Remember when JJ throw Goo in ocean fire?

Oh yeah – we thought you were dead!

HA HA HA HA

HA HA HA

Glad to hear you've come to your senses, chum.

Hey, what do you think happened to **Super Supreme?**

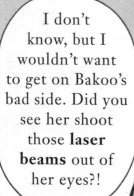

I don't know, but I wouldn't want to get on Bakoo's bad side. Did you see her shoot those **laser beams** out of her eyes?!

I certainly won't be losing any sleep over the fate of that **charlatan.**

Well, JJ, I bet you have lots of admin work to catch up on.

We'll see you at dinner, huh?

Nah, you were right, Flygirl. That stuff can wait. And besides . . .

151

The end.

And in case you missed them!

Super Sidekicks 1: No Adults Allowed

Super Sidekicks 2: Ocean's Revenge

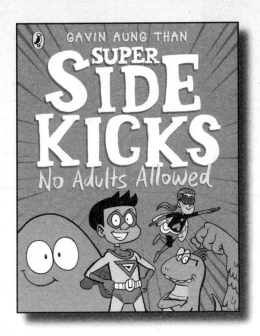

Grab your copies now!

GAVIN AUNG THAN is a *New York Times*-bestselling cartoonist and the creator of the Super Sidekicks. He once attempted the Trial of Heroes but got a heat rash in the desert and had to turn back before making it to the Temple of Champions.

VISIT GAV'S WEBSITE AT *AUNGTHAN.COM*

A SUPER THANK YOU to the team at Penguin Random House: Zoe W., Niki, Kate, Laura, Nerrilee, Dot, Jen, Jess B., Windle and Zoe B. Thanks also to my agent, Brian, and last but not least, to my amazing and supportive wife, Jessica. – GAV